This book belongs to

____

Written by Meredith Rusu
Designed by Cheung Tai

ISBN 978-1-338-67088-2

10 9 8 7 6 5 4 3 22 23 24 25

Printed in China 68
First printing 2021

GREETINGS, POKÉMON TRAINER

We have exciting news! YOU have been chosen to join Ash and Goh as they travel on an adventure through the Galar region. Congratulations!

Within these pages are three action-packed comics you'll use as your guide to discover the secrets of the Galar region. Along the way, keep the stickers and stencils handy as you solve puzzles, complete challenges, and even match wits against your friends.

Be prepared: the Galar region is filled with surprises big and small. You never know when a new Pokémon might sneak up on you—or grow ten times its size!

Are you ready to begin? Excellent. Grab a Poké Ball and turn the page.

YOUR JOURNEY STARTS . . . NOW!

STENCIL KEY

Here is the key to the type symbols that are on your stencils!

NORMAL	FIRE	WATER	GRASS	ELECTRIC	ICE

FIGHTING	POISON	GROUND	FLYING	PSYCHIC	BUG

ROCK	DRAGON	GHOST	DARK	STEEL	FAIRY

BIG SURPRISES

Ash and Goh are traveling through the Galar region in search of giant-sized Pokémon: Pokémon that have DYNAMAXED!

Snorlax. The Sleeping Pokémon. As it begins to eat, it falls asleep, and it sleeps while it eats. Its average height is a bit less than seven feet. The height of this Snorlax measures ten and a half feet.

Just then, Ash and Goh get a surprise visitor.
Scorbunny!
It's the Scorbunny they met the other day.
We know you!
Don't tell me you came looking for us?
Scorbunny!
I think it wants to be your partner!
Wow, you really mean it?

Scorbunny is heartbroken.

Strange red lights begin glowing around the sleeping Snorlax . . .

Could this be the mysterious Dynamax they've been looking for?

To be continued . . .

POKÉDEX POWER UP!

Ash and Goh are discovering lots of exciting surprises in the Galar region! Use your stickers and stencils to add details to the info they learned from Goh's Rotom Phone about the Pokémon they encountered.

SNORLAX

Category: Sleeping Pokémon

Type: Normal

Height: 6'11"

Weight: 1014.1 lbs.

Use your stencil to draw the symbol for Snorlax's type!

It is not satisfied unless it eats over 880 pounds of food every day. When it is done eating, it goes promptly to sleep.

SCORBUNNY

Category: Rabbit Pokémon

Type: Fire

Height: 1'00"

Weight: 9.9 lbs.

Use your stencil to draw the symbol for Scorbunny's type!

It has special pads on the backs of its feet, and one on its nose. Once it's raring to fight, these pads radiate tremendous heat.

THE HEAT IS ON!

Scorbunny must race across the Galar region to find Goh and become his Pokémon partner. Help it reach its goal by completing the maze below.

READY FOR ACTION!

Scorbunny, Grookey, and
Sobble are ready for action! Color the panels below.

CALLING ALL POKÉMON

Ten Pokémon are hidden in the word search below. Search up, down, across, diagonally, and backward to find and circle them.

BULBASAUR • CHARMANDER • FLAREON • EEVEE • GROOKEY
LUDICOLO • PIKACHU • SCORBUNNY • SOBBLE • SQUIRTLE

F	B	U	L	B	A	S	A	U	R	V	U	S	M
P	G	Q	B	I	D	L	A	E	S	U	B	S	I
P	V	Y	E	S	K	O	D	N	Q	Z	Y	C	L
U	E	B	W	J	A	N	O	Z	U	T	G	K	N
E	E	V	E	E	A	R	Y	X	I	R	B	H	S
L	D	Z	O	M	E	N	O	E	R	A	L	F	C
U	B	O	R	R	I	V	E	L	T	C	U	E	O
D	Y	A	X	W	G	P	X	I	L	O	W	M	R
I	H	A	L	P	R	M	R	U	E	K	T	I	B
C	V	I	S	U	O	N	P	I	K	A	C	H	U
O	J	T	W	S	O	B	B	L	E	I	W	B	N
L	Z	W	Q	J	K	D	U	B	T	S	O	N	N
O	P	S	U	M	E	W	I	Z	U	W	B	I	Y
P	S	U	N	A	Y	T	L	Q	U	V	F	A	N

SCRAMBLED UP

These Pokémon names have gotten all mixed up! Unscramble the names and then draw lines connecting them to their correct owner.

TUARHNE

____

UPLGYIJFGF

____

OASLBSITE

____

ZIRAHCDRA

____

ETNOOLJ

____

WHO'S THAT POKÉMON?

Connect the dots below to reveal the hidden Mythical Pokémon.

Use your stencils to draw the symbol for the hidden Pokémon's type!

Category: New Species Pokémon

Type: Psychic

Height: 1'4"

Weight: 8.8 lbs.

When viewed through a microscope, this Pokémon's short, fine, delicate hair can be seen.

PIKA-WHO?

Pikachu is squaring off against Mimikyu! Play Dots and Boxes with a friend to determine who will win. Have one player choose the Electric-type stickers for Pikachu, and the other the Ghost-type stickers for Mimikyu. Take turns drawing one horizontal or vertical line between the dots. If your line completes a box, place one of your stickers in the center, then go again. The player with the most completed boxes at the end wins.

Electric type **Ghost type**

COLOR BY NUMBER

Use the guide below to color in the picture of Thwackey!

Key:

1 = Light Green; **2** = Light Yellow; **3** = Orange; **4** = Brown; **5** = Dark Green; **6** = Dark Yellow

Leave any blank spots white

THWACKEY

Category: Beat Pokémon

Type: Grass

Height: 2'04"

Weight: 30.9 lbs.

The faster a Thwackey can beat out a rhythm with its two sticks, the more respect it wins from its peers.

Use your stencils to draw the symbol for Thwackey's type!

CLUES AND CODES

Use the key below to reveal a
secret message from Professor Cerise for Ash and Goh.

= A	= E	= I	= N	= R
= G	= H	= L	= O	= T

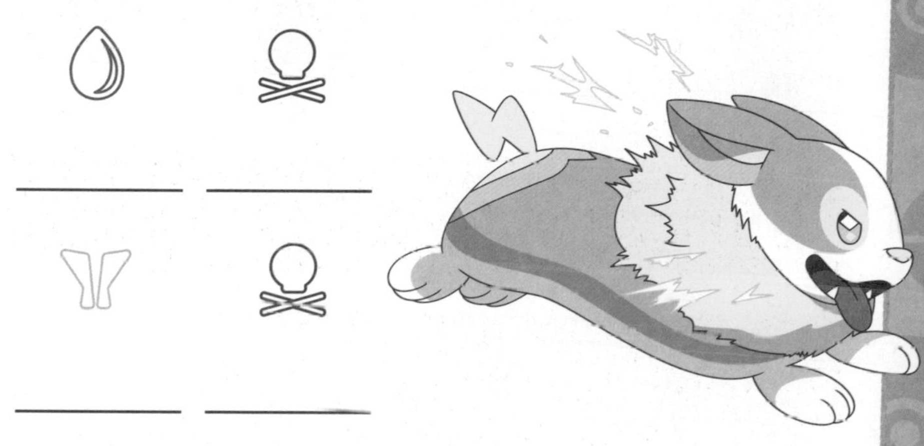

DYNAMAX TO THE MAX!

Ash and Goh watch as something BIG starts happening to Snorlax. Something . . . Dynamax!

Hey, Ash! Is this . . . ?

Who knows? Let's get out of here!

Snorlax grows bigger . . .

And bigger . . .
SCREEEEEEEEECH!

And bigger . . .
FWOOM!

Could it be? Is *this* Dynamax?
It's like a mountain! It's so big, and there's an actual tree up there!

It grew right over the railroad tracks!

And the next train is due in eight minutes!
Come on, Snorlax! Move! Hurry up! You've got to get out of here!

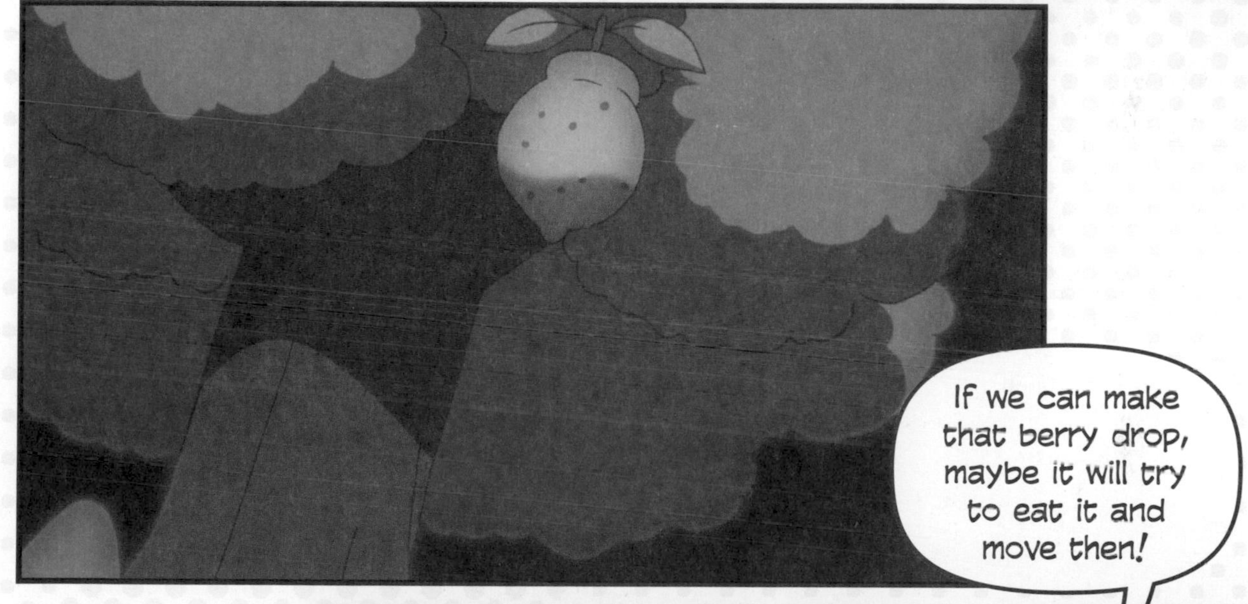

Will Goh and Ash's plan work? Can they get Snorlax to move out of the way in time?

To be continued . . .

SUPERSIZED

Dynamax Pokémon grow SUPER large! Choose your favorite Pokémon below and use the grid as a guide to draw that Pokémon Dynamax-sized on the next page!

SPOT THE DIFFERENCE

There are five differences between the two images below. Find and circle them.

MAJOR MIX-UP!

This picture has gotten all mixed up! Place the pieces of this image back in the correct order.

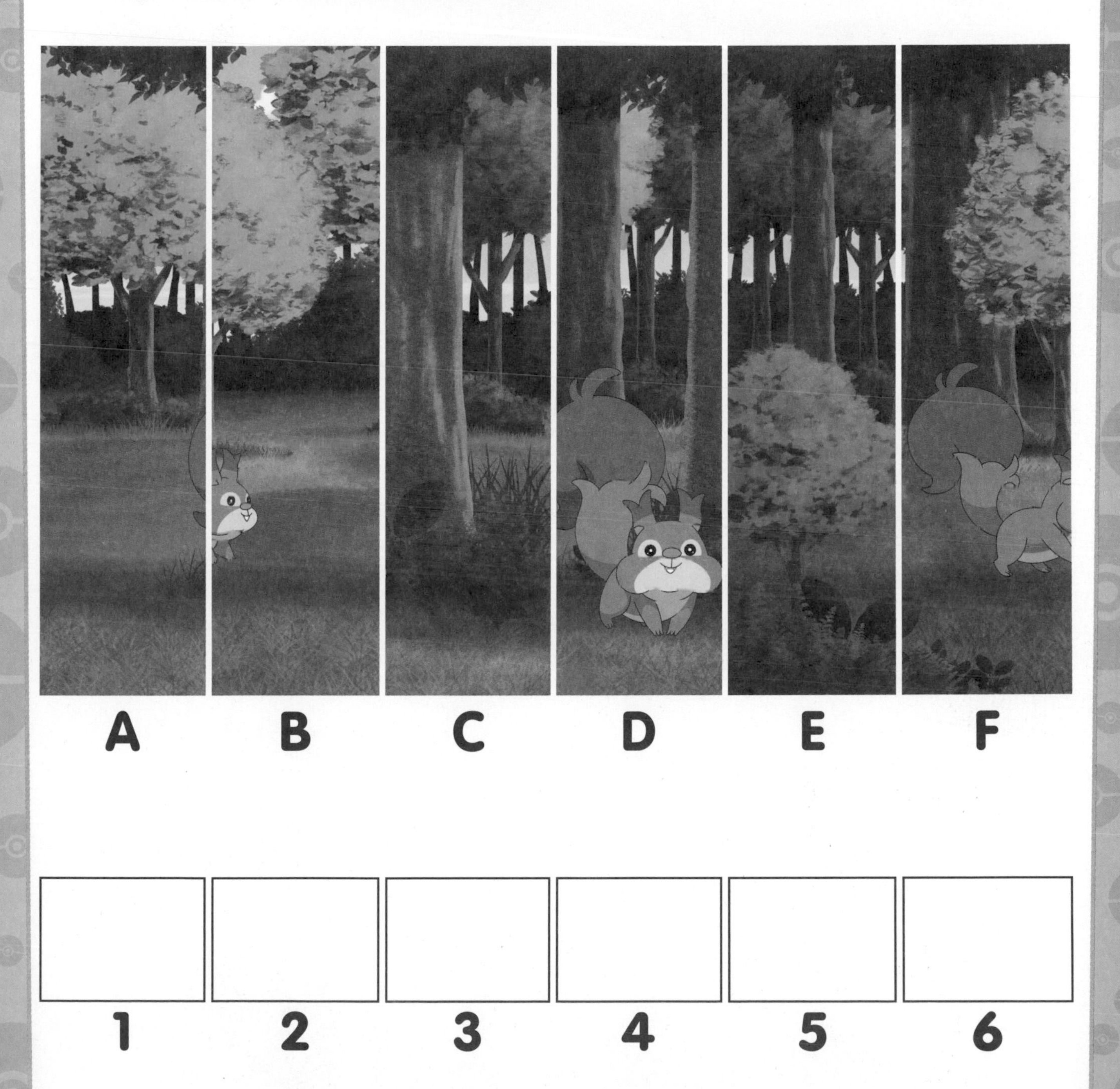

TYPE MATCH

Draw a line from each Pokémon to its type.

Dark

Electric

Bug

Fairy

Water

BEST BUDDIES

Pokémon friends are forever!
Color the panels of Squirtle, Bulbasaur, and Charmander below.

HIDDEN TYPES

Every known Pokémon type is hidden in the word search below. Search up, down, across, diagonally, and backward to find and circle them. Then decorate the page by using your type symbol stencils!

Bug • Dark • Dragon • Electric • Fairy • Fire • Fighting Flying • Ground • Grass • Ghost • Ice • Normal • Poison Psychic • Rock • Steel • Water

E	D	A	R	K	P	S	Y	C	H	I	C	X
L	W	R	N	S	O	G	Q	I	Z	H	S	T
E	Z	O	B	A	I	S	P	G	H	O	S	T
C	N	C	L	T	S	T	W	K	S	L	J	G
T	U	K	I	A	O	E	E	A	F	P	N	R
R	T	D	R	U	N	E	B	T	W	I	C	E
I	M	G	Q	V	K	L	C	B	Y	D	H	T
C	D	R	A	G	O	N	M	L	A	I	W	A
D	F	O	P	O	I	Y	F	A	I	R	Y	W
Z	X	U	V	B	N	M	I	O	I	U	Y	T
R	E	N	A	S	N	O	R	M	A	L	D	F
G	H	D	J	K	L	N	E	B	V	C	X	Z
T	F	I	G	H	T	I	N	G	J	G	U	B

TIC-TAC-TOGEPI

Play a game of Tic-Tac-Togepi with a friend! Choose either the blue triangle or red diamond stickers from the sticker sheets to be your symbol. Take turns placing a sticker in an empty space of the Tic-Tac-Togepi board. The first with three in a row wins!

WHO'S THAT POKÉMON?

Connect the dots below to reveal the hidden Pokémon.

Category: Two-Sided Pokémon

Type: Electric-Dark

Height: 1'00"

Weight: 6.6 lbs.

Use your stencils to draw the symbol for the hidden Pokémon's type!

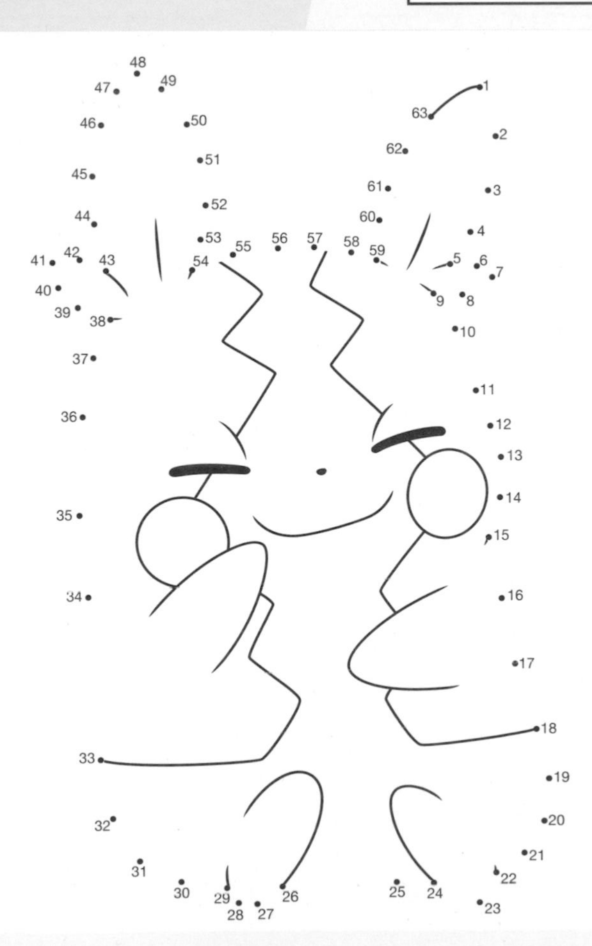

As it eats the seeds stored up in its pocket-like pouches, this Pokémon is not just satisfying its constant hunger. It's also generating electricity.

THE WAY HOME

Pikachu has gotten separated from Ash. Help the friends find each other by completing the maze below.

SCORBUNNY TO THE RESCUE!

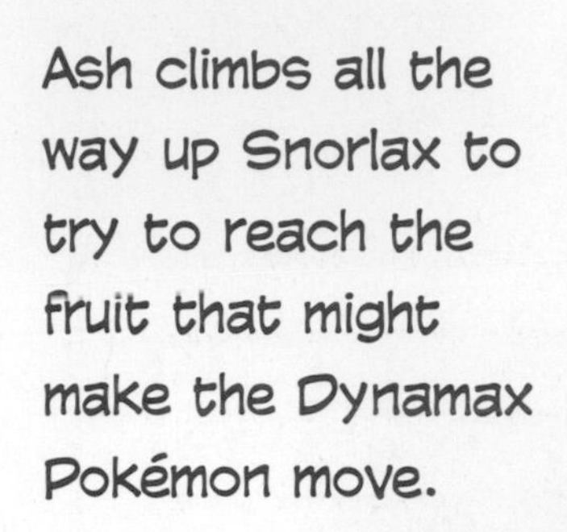

Pikachu!
Use Iron Tail
that way!

PIKAAAAAA . . .
CHUUUU!
SNAP!
All right!
Way to go!

But the fruit gets stuck!
Not there!
The fruit is too heavy to move.
Uuuuughhh!
And the train is almost here!

But just then . . . Scorbunny comes to the rescue!

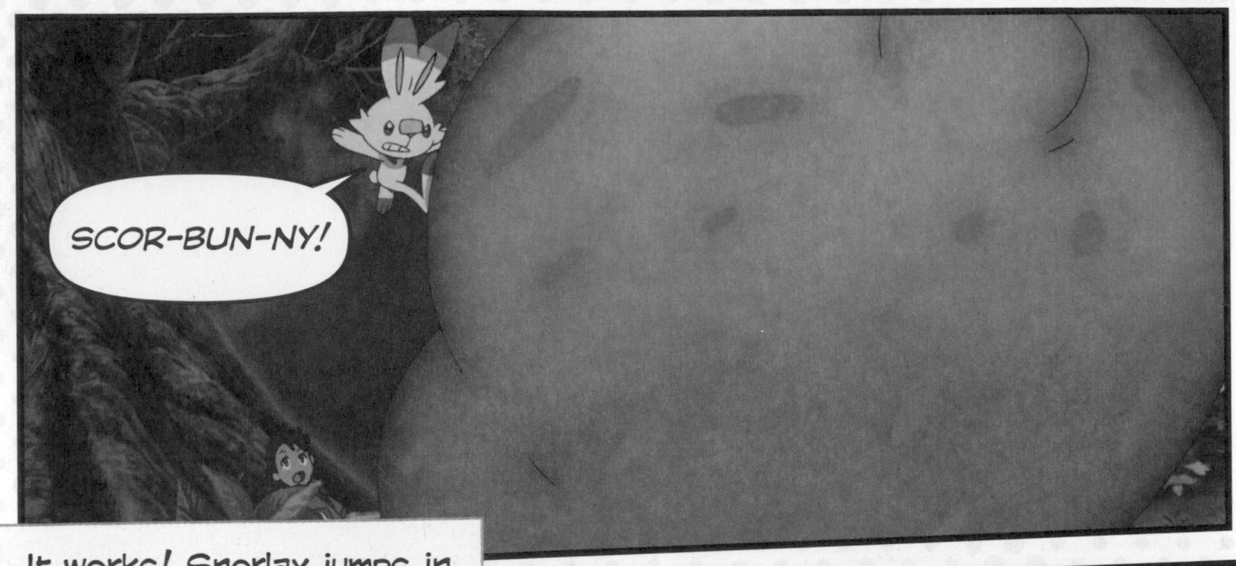

It works! Snorlax jumps in its sleep to eat the fruit!

The train track is cleared just in time!

Crisis averted! The Dynamax effect wears off, and Snorlax shrinks back down to its normal size.
Whoooooaaaa!
Scorbunny, you did it!
Your Double Kick saved everybody on that train!

Goh has learned that even the smallest Pokémon can bring the biggest surprises of all.

The end.

ODD ONE OUT

Even though Scorbunny is a little Pokémon, it has big spirit.
Which of these Scorbunny is not like the others?
Circle the odd one out.

YOUR FIRST POKÉMON

Which Pokémon would YOU want to catch first?
Draw a picture of you as a Pokémon Trainer catching your very first Pokémon below.

MEOWTH'S MATCH

Only one shadow of Meowth is the right one.
Circle the correct match!

HOW MANY WORDS?

List the words you can make out of the letters in . . .

TEAM ROCKET

POKÉMON PUZZLE

Use your stickers to fill in the missing pieces of the Pokémon puzzle below.

EVOLUTION REVOLUTION

Use your stickers to fill in the Evolution of each Pokémon below.

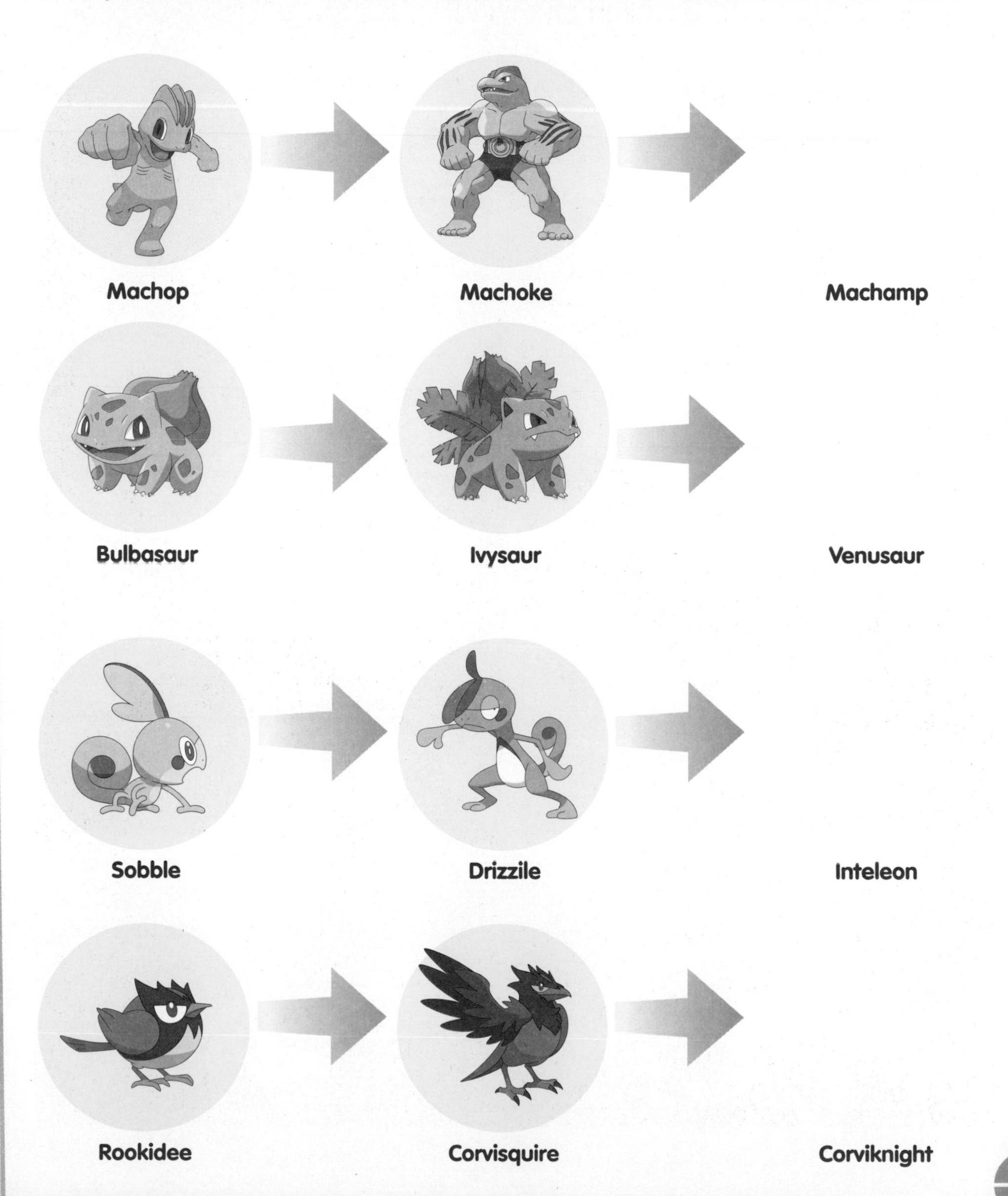

POKÉ BALL MADNESS

Pokémon Trainers have lost track of their Poké Balls in the forest! How many Poké Balls can you count in this picture?

PICK A PATH

Which path leads Ash and Pikachu to Goh and Scorbunny?

POKÉMON QUIZ

Use the knowledge you gained during your journey with Ash and Goh to answer these questions.

1. Which region are Ash and Goh traveling through?
   a. Johto
   b. Kalos
   c. Galar

2. What type of Pokémon are Ash and Goh looking for?
   a. Sleeping
   b. Dynamax
   c. Hungry

3. Snorlax's type is . . .
   a. Normal
   b. Fire
   c. Psychic

4. What does Scorbunny want to be?
   a. A hero
   b. Goh's partner
   c. A Dynamax Pokémon

5. What Pokémon does Goh want to catch first?
   a. Psyduck
   b. Snorlax
   c. Mew

6. The pads on Scorbunny's face and feet give off . . .
   a. A funny smell
   b. Laser beams
   c. Intense heat

7. How do Ash and Goh realize Snorlax is becoming Dynamax?
   a. Red lights start hovering around it
   b. It snores super loud
   c. It eats extra berries

8. What does Pikachu use to cut down the berry?
   a. Thunder Tail
   b. Iron Tail
   c. Sharp Teeth

9. What move does Goh tell Scorbunny to use to push the berry?
   a. Flaming Kick
   b. Thunder Kick
   c. Double Kick

10. Working together, the friends save . . .
   a. The train from crashing
   b. The train from waking up Snorlax
   c. The world

11. Who becomes Goh's first Pokémon?
   a. Mew
   b. Pikachu
   c. Scorbunny

ANSWER KEY

Page 10:

Page 12:

F B U L B A S A U R V U S M
P G Q B I D L A E S U B S I
P V Y E S K O D N Q Z Y C L
U E B W J A N O Z U T G K N
E E V E E A R Y X I R B H S
L D Z O M E N O E R A L F C
U B O R R I V E L T C U E O
D Y A X W G P X I L O W M R
I H A L P R M R U E K T I B
C V I S U O N P I K A C H U
O J T W S O B B L E I W B N
L Z W Q J K D U B T S O N N
O P S U M E W I Z U W B I Y
P S U N A Y T L Q U V F A N

Page 13:

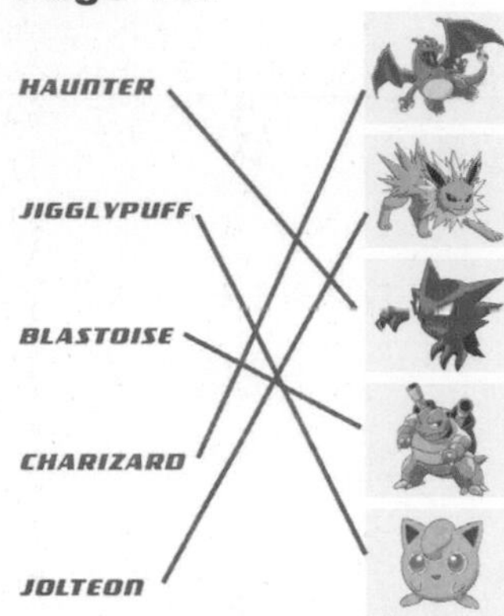

Page 14:

Mew

Page 17:

GO
TO
THE
GALAR
REGION

Page 24:

Page 25:

E F B A D C

Page 26:

Page 28:

E D A R K P S Y C H I C X
L W R N S O G Q I Z H S T
E Z O B A I S P G H O S T
C N C L T S T W K S L J G
T U K I A O E E A F P N R
R T D R U N E B T W I C E
I M G Q V K L C B Y D H T
C D R A G O N M L A I W A
D F O P O I Y F A I R Y W
Z X U V B N M I O I U Y T
R E N A S N O R M A L D F
G H D J K L N E B V C X Z
T F I G H T I N G J G U B

Page 30:

Morpeko

Page 31:

Page 39:

Page 41:

Page 44:

Answer: **35**

Page 45:

Answer: **B**

Page 46:

1. **c**
2. **b**
3. **a**
4. **b**
5. **c**
6. **c**
7. **a**
8. **b**
9. **c**
10. **a**
11. **c**